THE
BOOK
CAT

FABER has published children's books since 1929. T. S. Eliot's *Old Possum's Book of Practical Cats* and Ted Hughes' *The Iron Man* were amongst the first. Our catalogue at the time said that 'it is by reading such books that children learn the difference between the shoddy and the genuine'. We still believe in the power of reading to transform children's lives. All our books are chosen with the express intention of growing a love of reading, a thirst for knowledge and to cultivate empathy. We pride ourselves on responsible editing. Last but not least, we believe in kind and inclusive books in which all children feel represented and important.

THE
BOOK
CAT

Polly Faber

Illustrated by

Clara Vulliamy

faber

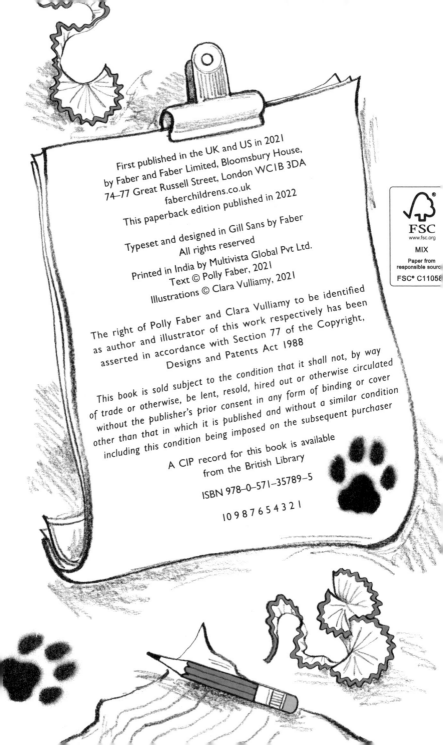

First published in the UK and US in 2021
by Faber and Faber Limited, Bloomsbury House,
74–77 Great Russell Street, London WC1B 3DA
faberchildrens.co.uk
This paperback edition published in 2022

Typeset and designed in Gill Sans by Faber
All rights reserved
Printed in India by Multivista Global Pvt Ltd.
Text © Polly Faber, 2021
Illustrations © Clara Vulliamy, 2021

The right of Polly Faber and Clara Vulliamy to be identified
as author and illustrator of this work respectively has been
asserted in accordance with Section 77 of the Copyright,
Designs and Patents Act 1988

A CIP record for this book is available
from the British Library

ISBN 978–0–571–35789–5

10 9 8 7 6 5 4 3 2 1

FSC
www.fsc.org
MIX
Paper from
responsible sourc
FSC® C11058

For all my book cats past and present –
Sid, Lupin, Daisy, Jones, Alan and Babs,
with love, respect and tuna,

PF

For my mum, who taught herself to write
and illustrate stories during the Liverpool Blitz,
in between queueing with her ration book and
knitting misshapen balaclavas for the troops.

CV

Dear Reader,

I am writing this book, as I write all my books, with the help of two cats. Alan, white and black and extremely fluffy, is on the floor in a huff because I scooped him out of my chair to sit at my desk. His sister Babs, black and white with a fine moustache, is beside my computer keyboard watching my mouse and occasionally pouncing on it when I move it. They will tell me when it's

1

time for lunch.

I'm not the only writer with cats. In fact
if you ask you'll find that most writers have a
cat or two. (Of course a few writers have dogs
instead of cats. I'm sure they also have excellent
qualities but Alan and Babs will not let me write
a word about them.) A connection between
cats and writing goes back a very long way: it's
no coincidence that cat hieroglyphs appear so
frequently on scraps of Egyptian papyrus or in
the corners of medieval manuscripts. I'm not sure

2

Alan and Babs are descended from the elegant sphinx cats of Ancient Egypt, but I sometimes wonder if they might be connected to an important Book Cat from more recent times.

When my father was a boy, his father ran a company that made books; it was called Faber and Faber. One of the people who worked there was a famous poet called T. S. Eliot and he was my father's godfather. T. S. Eliot loved cats and wrote funny poems about them in letters to my father and other children he knew. The rest of T. S. Eliot's poems were serious and very grown-up, but these funny poems turned out to be so good they were made into a book for everybody to enjoy. The book is called *Old Possum's Book of Practical Cats*.

The original poems in *Old Possum's Book of Practical Cats* were about imaginary cats but one poem, added a little later, is different from the others. It's based on a real cat; a stray called Morgan who turned up at Faber and Faber during the war and never left. Morgan was a completely black cat, a rather *large* cat, and he answered the door at Fabers for many years. Eliot told one story about him. As you'll read, I heard a slightly different one. But then every cat has nine lives.

One thing everyone can agree on is that Morgan was a truly dedicated Book Cat. In fact some might even say he invented the job . . .

BLITZ KITTEN

Morgan arrived the same night as the first enemy
bombers. His mother gave birth unexpectedly,
on the eastbound platform of the Piccadilly line
at Holborn station. She had not been waiting
for a train. As the sirens had begun to wail, she

7

had weaved between legs to join the stream of Londoners coming to seek shelter in the underground.

While humans shared stories and songs, trying to ignore what was happening above their heads, the skinny tortoiseshell cat had been unable to ignore that her kittens were coming. She had only just had time to make herself comfortable in a dark corner, on top of a felt hat and a folded copy of the *Evening News*.

Two kittens safely delivered, the new family spent their first night curled in a ball of milky happiness. The walls and ceiling hummed from distant explosions above ground but they didn't care. They were quite unnoticed, until the All Clear sounded and a lady came searching for her hat and newspaper: 'Oh my!'

The lady decided she didn't need either returned.

In later years Morgan wondered whether being born on to paper fixed his destiny – even such poor-quality paper as the wartime *Evening News* was printed on. It was certainly true that for ever after, the smell of ink made him feel safe and brought back the feeling of his mother's tongue rasping the top of his head clean, her throaty purrs vibrating even louder in his ear than the noise of the bombs. Of all the different beds he tried through his life, not even a pile of clean laundry could bring swifter, sweeter sleep than paper.

Black as a lump of coal, and not much bigger, Morgan stayed underground for his first few weeks of life, playing tail-tip-tag and pat-a-paw-pounce with his tabby-striped sister Maeve in the tunnels and stairwells of the station. Their mother

only left them to find dinner; mostly food scraps dropped by the people who took the trains by day and returned for shelter each night, but sometimes an unlucky tube-tunnel mouse who'd come to compete for the crumbs.

As the kittens grew and needed more than milk, the crusts of a paste sandwich or the corner of a cold fritter were not enough to feed them all. So one sharp frosty morning their mother led the kittens upstairs to see their city at last.

'Hello, Petal! Where have you been hiding?' A bruiser of a ginger tom greeted Morgan's mother on the street corner. The kittens stuck close by her and blinked and stared at their first sight of cars and buses and buildings and the pink-tinged winter sky.

'I've been a bit busy, Roly,' answered Petal, nudging Morgan and Maeve out from under the shelter of her legs. 'Say hello to your uncle, kittens.'

'Babies? You kept that quiet, Pet. Top-of-the-milk congratulations to you! Welcome to London, little ones. It's a fine time to be a cat in this city. It's always the best of cities, but it's better than ever in this war.'

'Even with the bombs, Roly? I've been so worried. The humans sheltering with us have moved their children out to the country. Don't you think I should do the same?'

'Go to the *country*? With pickings for cats as rich as they are now? You'd be three whiskers short of a sneeze if you did, Petal, take it from me: just head out east down to the docks and tell me if I'm wrong. They've been taking the worst of the bombs that way and you never saw better feasting. The sewers have been opened and there are rats running free all over the place. And the tumbled-down walls of every butcher, grocer and house give you larders free for the raiding. Grabbed myself a whole chicken pie yesterday. A whole pie!'

Morgan's eyes grew even wider, and he and Maeve stared up at their mother hopefully. They didn't know much about chicken or pies but they already knew what it was to have a belly that rumbled constantly for more than could fill it.

'I don't know, Roly. Is it safe down that way, if the city is in ruins?'

The ginger tom winked at the kittens. "Course it's safe if you keep your ears pricked and tail up. You've got nine lives, haven't you?'

'Please, Mamma. We're so hungry,' Maeve clamoured. Morgan pawed at his mother's shoulders and mewed pitifully. Their mother wavered. Before the end of the day the little trio had walked down to the great, murky River Thames and turned left to follow it east.

Roly wasn't wrong about the rich pickings. Not just pies but half-eaten stews, cold rice puddings, meat pasties – there was a feast for the cats if they looked hard enough. Over the next days, as they moved further into the East End, they came across more and more damaged houses; walls missing, doors gone, or entirely reduced to rubble. Whatever had happened to the occupants, they'd left in a hurry and there

16

were often the remnants of an abandoned meal to be sniffed out.

'Eat every scrap now. Shame to let it spoil,' Petal directed her babies as she rescued a piece of fish or pulled out a hunk of ham for them.

As the days went by, the kittens grew a little plumper. Their coats became glossier. Days became weeks and they weren't babies any longer. They grew braver and more boisterous in the playground of ruined buildings.

'Can't catch
me, slow-paws!'

Maeve would tease her brother, jumping off a
window ledge and racing away: she was always
the first to start any game. Morgan would give
chase, hurtling after his sister across the piles
of tumbledown bricks and burnt beams. Maeve
would get far enough ahead to hide under a
collapsed door or broken pipe and then leap
out to surprise Morgan. Then there would be
a somersault of claws and hisses, which would
quickly collapse into a bundle of licks and purrs
before a new game began. 'My silly pair of fur-
crackers,' Petal called them fondly.

After dark, when the sirens sounded, the
three cats sought shelter in Underground stations,
cuddled up to each other, or found refuge in
cellars. Sometimes they even sneaked inside one
of the corrugated metal Anderson shelters people
had dug into their gardens. They felt quite safe,
just as Roly had promised. But night after night
through the spring of 1941 the enemy bombers
returned, using the moonlit thread of the
River Thames to guide them in to drop their
deadly loads.

Morgan didn't see it happen. He was
distracted by a butterfly. It landed on the tip of
his nose and woke him from the delicious nap
he'd been taking in the May sunshine, curled on
a wall with his mother and sister. Opening his
eyes and seeing a pair of scarlet wings fluttering,
Morgan batted out at it and fell right off the wall.
Excited by the opportunity to catch something

ahead of his sister, he gave chase as the butterfly danced off ahead of him down the street. So intent was he, Morgan didn't hear the engine overhead. He didn't see the dark shape falling from the sky. He didn't look back until after the explosion had sent him flying up right into the butterfly and knocked both of them back on to the ground with the rest of the rubble and dust.

When he did look back, he saw the wall was gone. And so were his mother and sister.

CAT BURGLAR

Morgan knew there had to be *something* worth
stealing at the War Fair. It had been two years
since the loss of his mother and sister. And still
the war dragged on and on. The days of rich
pickings for any young cat on the make were

gone. Human food was tightly rationed now and that meant little waste and next to no scraps in the bins.

By means lawful and not so lawful Morgan had learned to get by on his own; in no small part thanks to all he had learned playing games with Maeve. But there was no trace any more of the plump kitten, and his coat was no longer glossy. No matter what he scavenged, Morgan was *always* hungry.

The fair was being held in Russell Square – streets of tall houses, elegant office buildings and grand hotels bordering a park shaded by trees where soldiers courted their sweethearts and office

workers relaxed. In this space, stalls had been set up for a carnival to raise money for the war effort.

It was a warm Saturday in June and despite the worry of the war there was a party atmosphere. Morgan's keen nose twitched. He was sure he could smell an opportunity. The scrawny young cat weaved unnoticed through the crowd of people – some had come to play games, others to listen to a brass band and cheer on the troops. But it was a man on stage in the middle of the square who attracted Morgan's attention. The man was holding something in his hand and people were gathered around, pointing and

murmuring. Stealthily, Morgan approached

and snuck up on to the back of the stage.

'A most rare and exotic treat!' the man

explained. 'Imagine introducing your children to

their first ever taste of this fabulous . . . BANANA!'

There was a chorus of *Oohs* from his audience.

Morgan inched closer, his whiskers quivering. 'It

is my privilege to auction off this much-sought-

after item today, ladies and gentlemen!' the man

continued. 'When will we see its like again? Are

your mouths watering? Dig deep in your pockets!

Who will start me off at three shillings?'

A banana? It didn't *look* like much; so small and greenish . . . but Morgan knew looks could be deceptive when it came to food. A tin of corned beef didn't look like much before it was opened. He crept closer. He was practically underneath the man.

'Five pounds, sir? I say, that *is* a handsome offer! What do we say, ladies and gentlemen, any advance on five pounds to aid our brave boys and girls overseas?' The auctioneer waved the banana again. 'One banana at five pounds, going once . . . going twice . . . going . . .'

With a daring he hoped Maeve would have been proud of, Morgan clawed straight up the man's trouser leg and pounced, grabbing the banana.

'WHAT? Ouch! I say . . . Hey! Stop that . . . *cat*!' yelled the man. 'STOP, THIEF!'

But Morgan was too fast. Holding his prize in his mouth, he set off through the legs of the

crowd, dodging grabbing hands, jumping under
and over the brass band, running across the
knees of the tuba player. He bounded straight
up a tree.

There was no time to stop and eat: the
crowd were up for the chase. An off-duty soldier
began climbing up on his comrade's shoulders
at the foot of the tree. They were laughing but
Morgan didn't doubt their intentions. He edged
along a branch which overhung the road. As the
number 19 bus came past, he shut his eyes and,
still gripping the banana, jumped, landing on the
roof with a THUMP!

The noise immediately alerted the conductor. She pulled on her cord to stop the bus.

A couple of soldiers were now out in front, pointing and laughing. 'Stop him! Grab that cat!'

Morgan raced across the roof, slid down the windscreen, off the bonnet and dropped to the ground. He darted round the corner, and passing

a grand white doorway, saw
a drainpipe leading up to a
low roof with more pipework
and upper storeys above it.
The crowd were nearly upon
him but he was a practised
rooftopper, so he leaped up
and kept climbing. Higher
and higher Morgan travelled,
until the rumble of his tummy
became louder than the
soldiers' shouts below. Only
when he was at the very top
did he finally stop to draw
breath and investigate his
dinner.

It took Morgan some time and all his claws to work out how to open the banana. He took a large bite – and spat it straight out. What was THAT!? His yowl of disappointment could have been heard as far as St Paul's Cathedral. All that effort for a piece of FRUIT! Outraged, and still hungry, Morgan curled up on the roof and prepared for another empty-belly night. He cleaned his whiskers and found not so much as a crumb hiding in them. But, just before he closed his eyes, he heard a noise coming from directly underneath him; the telltale scrabble-scuffling of mice in the room below!

Gingerly, Morgan climbed up the chimney stack and quietly put his head into one of the pots. He listened again. Yes! Mice! And more than one of them.

It was just as well he was skinny. He dropped into the chimney pot and tumbled down the flue, somersaulting out into the fireplace below in a shower of soot. His descent was fast enough that he kept the necessary element of surprise . . . Soon his belly was full, and with a much tastier dinner than a banana.

It was only when he'd finished that Morgan

realised he might be in a new sort of trouble. The door of the room he was in was shut. And getting back up out of a chimney proved to be harder than falling down it, especially now he'd eaten.

Morgan looked around. In the middle of the room was a big table. It was covered in piles of paper; paper that the mice had been chewing – his favourite sort of bed!

Morgan jumped on top of the fattest pile; it was delightfully smooth, cool and sweet-smelling.

He curled up and shut his eyes, suddenly feeling
as if his mother and Maeve were quite close by.
In no time at all Morgan was deeply asleep.

DOOR CAT

JUNE–OCTOBER 1943

'Aaaargh! We've got an alley cat in here. Brought half the chimney with it!' The woman brandished a broom. 'Get away with you, horrible animal! Shoo . . . SHOO!'

It wasn't the first time Morgan had been caught somewhere he wasn't supposed to be. He prepared to make his usual speedy exit through the woman's legs and down the stairs, but there was a man blocking his path.

The man bent down and picked a piece of paper up off the floor. It was one of several that had been decorated with sooty paw prints during Morgan's chase for mice the previous night. Ignoring the paper's crumpled state, the man took it to the armchair and stared at it.

'Well, look at that – wait, Mrs Lister: I think that cat may have solved a sticking point in stanzas three and five that has been troubling me for some time. Yes . . .' the man looked up and smiled at Morgan, 'you're absolutely right. If I remove the end of each line and run it on, then . . .' He got a pencil out of his pocket and began making quick marks on the paper. 'A Jellicle cat indeed! I'd say a saucer of milk is in order.' He reached out a hand to stroke behind Morgan's ear and Morgan decided to accept this tribute. He also decided that if a saucer of milk was on offer it would make a welcome breakfast before he left.

'At least he's been mousing.' The woman was sweeping up, and looked at the contents of her dustpan thoughtfully. 'Mr Faber will be thankful, what with paper being on ration. He was complaining only last week how mice keep nibbling away at the stores.'

'It might be time Faber and Faber had its own Practical Cat, don't you think, Mrs Lister? I'll speak with Geoffrey. This fellow might bring us luck, given his colour.' The man stroked the underside of Morgan's chin and Morgan stretched up his neck appreciatively.

The woman gave a sigh. 'We could all do with some of that, Mr Eliot.'

And that was how his next life began. Morgan found himself offered a roof over his head, not to mention a bowl with his name on and a title to earn his keep: Resident Mouser and Door Cat for publishing company Faber and Faber. What *was* a publishing company? It had to do with paper, but Morgan soon discovered it also had to do with people called *authors* and *editors*.

Every morning from nine on the dot, Morgan would take up position on the polished front step and oversee the arrival of that day's hopeful *authors*. They could be men or women, young or old, smartly or shabbily dressed; but all arrived clutching a stack of papers under their arm and with an air of jumpiness about them that at first made Morgan think they must be troubled by fleas. They would go in to see an *editor* and be closeted for a while. Then they would come out either with a shrug and slumped shoulders, still clutching their papers, or without them and sporting a huge grin.

Morgan decided that editors in a publishing company must cure fleas, as the authors seemed to lose their fidgetiness after seeing them. But after further study he discovered that, fleas aside, the authors also brought stories and the editors were choosing which to turn into *books*. Despite the war people still wanted books; stories, it seemed, could fill people up and satisfy them in the same way a pair of kippers satisfied Morgan. With this new-found understanding, the cat thoughtfully began to apply himself to helping the editors of Faber and Faber choose their authors wisely.

Any author who was disrespectful – who ignored Morgan's questioning 'Miaow?' or stepped on his tail or, on one terrible occasion, tried to kick him out of the way – was given *very* short shrift. But those who learned his name and who spent some time giving attention to the spot behind his ears – they were ushered straight inside. And those who brought *gifts*, a little something from a country larder that could supplement normal rations perhaps, Morgan saw up to the editor's office and stayed with until their manuscript had been definitely accepted.

With these rules understood, Morgan's fame spread and authors began to arrive prepared. On one particularly successful day Morgan helped

oversee the acceptance of an avant-garde volume
of poetry, a thrilling murder mystery and a tender
love story thanks to the thoughtful provision of a
fresh trout, a portion of rabbit stew and a pot
of cream.

Now Morgan fattened up again, and
his whiskers and fur gleamed. His grander
proportions seemed to befit a cat of new status,
although he would have struggled to fit down
a chimney pot.

The other cats of Russell Square observed his progress. There could have been jealousy but Morgan hadn't forgotten what it felt like to be hungry. A few weeks after starting his job he strolled through the square at dusk, climbed on to the dustbin that was their usual gathering place and made a speech.

'I know there's been some whisker-twitching and tail-thrashing in the alley about my new job, but never let it be said that I'm a cat to hoard the cream. Once a street cat, always a street cat, and it would honour the memory of my dear lost ma and sister if you'd let me share my fortune. There's a gap in the grating cover down in my basement that the mice have been using. Tonight I invite you to come through it yourselves. And I can promise that no cat will leave empty-pawed . . .'

That night, under the cover of blackout, a few curious cats accepted Morgan's invitation and found their way into the basement of 24 Russell Square. They were greeted with a magnificent spread of cold cutlets, custard and potted shrimp followed by a free-for-all mouse hunt. The boxes of books stacked around made perfect soundproofing: the resident caretaker didn't hear a thing.

After that more hungry cats turned up at the basement gap every night to see what was on offer. Word spread to all corners of London: Morgan, the big black cat at the smart painted doors, would offer waifs and strays a solid meal when needed. As autumn became winter, and the nights grew colder, the cats stayed longer. They shared stories and then, as can be expected when cats gather after dark, music. It wasn't long before Morgan found he was minding two different doors: a publishing house by day and –

by night – a caterwauling club. Morgan called it The Cat's Pyjamas.

The Cat's Pyjamas – what an atmosphere! What a place! Old-timers and kittens, tabby, tortoiseshell, tuxedo or ginger; as the war went on and 1943 turned into 1944 they came, in all shapes and sizes, to forget their worries with a song and a dance. They jived and they swung, and at the centre of it all was Morgan, now a cat in his prime; glossy and strong; a cat of real consequence.

But sometimes Morgan would disappear from his party and step out of his club. He'd gaze up at the stars above. He was a lucky cat. He'd found the good life. He knew it. But he still ached for what – *who* – he'd lost.

UNCLE CAT

JUNE 1944

Once the day's office business had drawn to a close, Morgan liked to wander across the park and find a quiet spot to catch the last rays of sun. By the summer of 1944 the square was quieter than it had been for some time. The American soldiers who'd arrived in huge numbers through the winter and spring had now left abruptly to fight in France. Morgan would curl on what little grass remained, close his eyes and have a nap before it was time to open The Cat's PJs for its long night of merriment.

No sooner had Morgan settled down for his snooze than a flurry of kittens arrived to use him as a climbing frame.

'Uncle Morgy! Uncle Morgy! Have you got us some grub? Please say you have.'

'Hmmm?' Morgan opened one eye. 'I don't know, Mimi. I might have . . .' He raised a paw and revealed the surprise they knew he had for them.

'PILCHARDS!'

'Share them nicely. And then wash your bibs and whiskers before your ma catches you.'

'We will, Uncle Morgy! Thank you, Uncle Morgy!'

'I've also got some pate for the Pyjamas later – Ow! Who's chewing my ear? Not *again*, Jumble. What are you doing up there?'

'I can see the whole world from the top of your head, Uncle Morgan! I wish I was big like you!' said a tortoiseshell with surprisingly sharp claws.

'Get down, eat your pilchards, then you'll grow,' directed a tiny tabby kitten who'd just arrived. She cuffed at another kitten crouching round the back. 'Uncle Morgan doesn't want you pouncing on his tail either, Winston.'

'Hello, Lou-Lou,' Morgan greeted the tabby fondly. Of all the new kittens who'd been born that spring in Russell Square, Lou-Lou was Morgan's favourite. Something about her stripes and fierce attitude reminded him sweet-sharp of his sister. 'Will your mum be singing tonight?' he asked. 'I've not seen her today.' Glamour-puss Peaches was one of the most popular artistes at The Cat's Pyjamas.

'I don't know, Uncle Morgy,' said Lou-Lou. 'She left me in charge because we lost our great-great-great-great-grandpa last night. She's gone to pay her respects.'

'Old Socks? Was it his heart?' Morgan stretched out his two front legs and flexed his toes. He'd known that battle-scarred tom well; a brave alley scrapper who'd lived through all sorts of adventures.

'No. Ma said it was some sort of new flying bomb caught him down Regent's Park way.'

A BOMB? Morgan sat bolt upright and stared at Lou-Lou as Jumble slid off his back. He'd almost been able to forget the humans' war over the last year but now the memories came flooding back. 'What?'

Lou-Lou looked surprised. 'Don't worry, Uncle Morgy, Socks was on to his last life. *We'll* all be fine.'

But now Morgan was staring at something else; at a scarlet butterfly fluttering just above Lou-Lou's head . . .

Over the next few nights, Morgan heard more and more tales of fresh bombs. They were different from the first lot that had been dropped from planes. These bombs had their own motors. They could arrive anywhere, at any time, the only warning a whining buzz overhead: *Weaaaaaaaaaaaaaaah*. When the noise stopped the bomb would drop.

The other cats in the square were unconcerned. 'We've got nine lives. It won't affect us, Morgan.'

But nine lives weren't always enough, as Morgan knew.

Each night distant booming reached them and the basement walls shook. The cats sang more loudly than ever, while the humans from the offices above took turns on the roof keeping watch in case of fire. Morgan joined them in scanning the skies. He was determined that he would not be distracted a second time.

It was a fortnight later, and the humans had all gone home to their beds when Morgan finally caught the noise he'd been dreading: an unmistakable buzzing whistle directly overhead. He raced down the drainpipe to squeeze back through to The Cat's Pyjamas. He just had time to yowl a warning to the others before the explosion.

There was a massive noise of glass crashing, ceilings and walls tumbling and the world turning inside out. Then a moment of shocked silence, broken by pitiful mewling inside, and by sirens and screams outside.

A large part of the building was damaged, and the basement ceiling had come down. Black, white, tabby, ginger; whatever colour they'd been at the beginning of the night, every cat had been turned grey with plaster and dust. One by one they picked themselves up and,

shaking and silent, began to leave the basement, a silvery river of cat ghosts streaming out through the gap.

Morgan checked and counted every cat as they exited: Fifteen . . . sixteen . . . he kept scanning for one family in particular . . . seventeen . . . eighteen . . . For a moment it seemed as if the ginger tom might be the last; Morgan paced back and forth anxiously. *Finally* Peaches emerged with her kittens.

With *three* of her kittens . . .

'Have you seen Lou-Lou?' she asked Morgan, looking around her.

Morgan's whiskers tingled and his fur bristled. 'She's not come out,' he said. 'She must still be inside somewhere. Peaches, I'll find her . . .' Morgan turned and plunged back into the darkness of the collapsed building.

Even with cat's eyes it was hard to see through the thick dust in the basement. Morgan shook his head to get rid of the crumbs of plaster falling on his whiskers. 'Lou-Lou?' he called. Outside there were shouts and cries and

sirens but inside was eerily silent. 'Lou-Lou?'
he called again.

Morgan's heart was pounding; if something
had happened to that kitten he wouldn't be able
to bear it. First his sister, now . . . He began to
sniff and paw under the lumps of plaster that had
fallen. They weren't particularly heavy but Lou-
Lou was only small. It wouldn't have taken much
to squash her . . .

From the far corner of the basement came
the tiniest of sneezes and the faintest of mews.

'Lou-Lou!' Morgan raced to the sound. It was
coming from a box of books.

'Uncle Morgy?'

Lou-Lou was alive! But she was trapped. She'd had the narrowest of escapes.

'I jumped inside when you shouted your warning, Uncle Morgy. Only now I can't seem to get out again.' A giant piece of plaster cornicing was wedged right across the box, jamming the lid shut.

It was lucky that Morgan was now a cat of such magnificent size. He bent his head and managed to work his shoulders under one end of the cornicing. 'Get ready to jump,' he urged. With a massive heave, he levered up the weight and released the pressure on the lid. '*Now, Lou-Lou!*'

Lou-Lou slithered out of the gap just as Morgan found he could no longer hold the weight and the cornicing collapsed again. There were more rumblings above.

'More of it's coming down,' said Morgan, looking up at the ceiling. 'Quick!' They both ran for the grating gap. Morgan shoved Lou-Lou through with his nose and then squeezed through himself.

'Uncle Morgy, you saved my life; *loads* of my lives,' said Lou-Lou. 'It was you and your books!'

PLANNER CAT

JUNE 1944

In daylight, everybody could see the full damage
to their homes. The rocket bomb had fallen bang
in the middle of Russell Square. The whole grass
area was now a crater. Every tree had been
blackened and lost its leaves and not a single

building facing the square had kept its front door or windows.

'Our box under the bench – it's disappeared. The *bench* has disappeared. If we hadn't been down in the basement . . .' Lou-Lou was saucer-eyed and trembling.

Peaches, in the middle of licking the dust off her kitten's coat, raised her head. 'I'm sure there won't be *another* bomb, Lou.'

But behind them, Mr Lister the caretaker was dragging suitcases on to the street from his flat next door to the offices. Mrs Lister was right behind him, with a toddler on each hip.

'I've spoken to my mother. The twins can't be living here with this nonsense starting up again,' Mrs Lister was saying to Miss Swan, the office receptionist.

Morgan watched the family. He thought of Lou-Lou's small mew in the dusty basement the previous night. He thought of another kitten who had not had the chance to grow up. 'We can't run the risk,' he said suddenly, turning to Peaches.

'What are you talking about, Uncle Morgy?' asked Lou-Lou.

'This time we need to get you out – get *all* of the kittens safely out of London,' said Morgan decisively. 'Sing the word out. If kittens are grown enough to leave their ma and their ma wants them to have the chance for a better life, well, let's just say I've got an idea . . .'

Word spread further than Morgan anticipated. That evening an excitable queue of cats and their kittens formed outside what was left of The Cat's Pyjamas. Morgan was a little overwhelmed by the numbers, so Lou-Lou took charge, even though some of the oldest kittens were twice her size.

She hissed and cuffed stragglers and scrappers back into place, and nose-rubbed and licked the ears of those who looked anxious. 'Don't worry, Uncle Morgy has a PLAN. It's something to do with his books. *Listen* to Uncle Morgy.'

Morgan had been expecting to get no more than ten, so he was surprised to find himself sole parent in charge of first sixteen . . . then

twenty . . . and finally – 'Are we too late?' –
twenty-three kittens! In addition to those around
the square he already knew well, there were
others who'd travelled a distance.

There were five-month-old twins Titch and
Tiny, who were definitely neither; Tom, Dick
and Harry, three fierce tabby kittens from the
butcher's at Holborn; an elegant Siamese named
Pearl who'd been brought all the way from

Mayfair; and an entirely ginger
litter whose mother handed
each one over by the scruff

with a large

fish apiece:

they'd come off a barge

on the Regent's Canal.

Morgan's tail tip twitched nervously. He had
a plan; it was a good plan, he hoped – but he
hadn't banked on needing to find homes for *so
many* kittens! There was no point in wasting time
worrying. He had to put his first stage into action:
hiding the kittens safely before the staff arrived for
work. With the basement ceiling destroyed, the
kittens needed to be stowed in the main offices.

Morgan got busy. From the bottom of the
building to the top, he deposited kittens in hidey-
holes on shelves and in desk tidies,

under cushions, inside galoshes

 and behind

carriage

 clocks.

Lou-Lou trotted beside
him like a shadow, helping to spot good hiding
places when he ran out of ideas. 'What about
those boxes, Uncle Morgy? We all like boxes!'
and Morgan found she was right; boxes for paper

and books were one thing the publisher's office had in plentiful supply. As he stowed away each kitten he instructed them to stay still, keep quiet and stay out of trouble.

'I don't expect they *will*, Uncle Morgy. I don't think that they can!' Lou-Lou said, with a casual flick of her tail. 'The trouble is kittens don't know how to. They'll cause all sorts of trouble.'

It had been a long night and there would be a long day ahead. Morgan turned to his bossy assistant and picked Lou-Lou up by her scruff. 'Lead by example, Lou-Lou. The instruction goes for you too,' he said. Ignoring her mews of protest but with a comforting goodbye lick, he posted her into the office teapot.

'What *is* the matter with Morgan? That cat doesn't normally stir once he's in a sunny spot but today he's *everywhere*. Look!' said Miss Swan, as Morgan darted through her chair at the switchboard, spinning her round. 'You're tangling my cables, Morgan — away with you!'

'Tangling seems to be rather in the air today,'

said Miss Sheldon the secretary, pulling a knotted lump of wool and unravelled knitting from her bag. She inspected it in bafflement. 'How strange; I can't think *how* this has happened since this morning. I'm afraid the troops will have to wait longer for their socks.'

'These horrid rocket attacks have unsettled us,' said Miss Swan. 'I'll make a nice pot of tea. Now what's the matter, Morgan? . . . MORGAN!'

Thanks to Morgan scattering the contents of a pen holder, neither of the women spotted kittens making speedy exits from rubbish bin, knitting and brown china teapot.

Somehow or other Morgan got to the end of the day.

'That,' said an exhausted Morgan to the twenty-three kittens sitting on the

office carpet, 'was the wor . . . the *second* worst day of all my lives. Now listen up, you . . . you . . .' he remembered his mother, 'silly bunch of fur-crackers. Everyone's gone home now, so you can be as noisy as you like, but *today* – well, your mas would be ashamed of you. If I'm to keep you safe, then you're going to need to *listen*! And settle down! And *study*! Park and alley manners are not going to cut it where I'm sending you.'

Lou-Lou was fidgety and bumptious after her day inside the teapot. 'Pah to that, Uncle Morgy. I don't want to be sent anywhere anyway. I'll take my chances on

81

the streets. Who wants to be a sleepy old house or office cat like *you*?' She stuck out the tip of her tongue and the other kittens grumbled in agreement.

Morgan puffed himself up to twice his usual size and hissed with unexpected firmness. Instantly the room quietened down; even Lou-Lou looked at her paws, abashed.

'Sleepy old house cat? SLEEPY OLD HOUSE CAT? Bombs or no bombs, have any of you the first idea what it's like to live on the streets?'

The kittens slowly shook their heads.

'I don't mean now, when the sun's out and your mas have been hunting all hours to make sure you don't go without. I mean through the weeks of winter when you're alone and your fur's soaked from ears to tail, so your very bones are cold and you haven't seen so much as a mackerel skin for days.' Morgan stared at them and then deflated a little.

'Anyway, I'm not talking about you being house cats. I've had a much better idea. You, if you'll all only apply yourselves, are going to be BOOK Cats. You are going to go and live with real live authors. You're going to help them write *much* better books than they'd manage without you – brilliant stories that everyone will love – and I'm going to teach you all I've learned. Now sit on your tails, prick up your ears and concentrate. Tonight we start the next part of my plan and that means *studying*.'

PRINCIPAL CAT

JUNE 1944

Morgan's impromptu school had much ground to cover. 'If you work hard, you'll find a writer's home is one where there's always milk for their

coffee in the larder and a
fireside that stays warm late
into the night. You'll be lucky
cats, safe from bombs now and forever. You'll
make me and your mothers proud,' he explained
the first night, pacing the length of an office desk.
The kittens were agog.

On Monday,

Morgan

taught the kittens
the cat's role as First
Editor: how to pounce
on and destroy a poor

piece of writing with claws, teeth or muddy
paws, and how to retrieve a good piece that

had been overlooked. This he demonstrated by showing them how to tip a bin over, select a crumpled ball and bat it back under a writer's nose for fresh consideration. They all practised, but as Tom, Dick and Harry became rather too inclined to turn it into a game of pawball Morgan quickly moved on.

On Tuesday, he showed them the many different faces of an unhappy writer and the meaning of their sighs. The

87

kittens learned basic distraction techniques: 'If a writer has just been at their desk too long, it's best for them to stretch their legs by way of the fridge or larder. So let's hear your best hungry mewling . . .' instructed Morgan. All the kittens showed great promise at this.

'If they're still looking sad after a trip to the fridge, they may have received something terrible called a Rejection Letter. Then you'll need to find ways to encourage them to give you a good stroke until they're able to write again,' Morgan explained.

It was no surprise to Morgan to see Lou-Lou was especially full of ideas for how that might be managed. She came up with a very tender way of nuzzling under a chin to soothe. He made all the other kittens gather to watch and copy her.

After these skills had been mastered there were further lessons in bookshelf dusting, and in typewriter return and ribbon change on Wednesday and Thursday, and windy-day paper-weighting and cold-weather lap-warming on Friday.

By the weekend, Morgan felt like he might be getting somewhere. The brightest kittens were really applying themselves. Even the slightly slower of his pupils might have to take their chances. Morgan could wait no longer. Although no further bombs had fallen directly on Russell Square, every night their lessons had been interrupted by distant telltale rumbling. Every day the chances of kitten discovery in the office increased too. The kittens needed to be sent on somewhere safer, and without any more delay.

On Sunday morning, Morgan lined them all up for one final test. He patrolled up and down his recruits.

90

'What's the first rule for a Book Cat?' he began, turning to a bright marmalade-orange fluffball in the front row; one of the barge kittens.

'To keep words under control just like mice.'

'That's right, Spitfire. Fewer words is better words. Without your help, writers will keep sitting and sighing and spilling their silliness for hours on end and it doesn't do them any good. So how are you going to make yours take a break, Sasha?'

'I thought I'd jump straight on their lap, chirrup and play pat-a-cake,' said a tubby brown kitten with a white bib.

'Very good.' Morgan twitched his tail approvingly and turned to a black kitten with white feet. 'And if that doesn't work? What else could you try, Mittens?'

'I could jump on to their desk, walk across and swipe papers and pencils off with my tail,' said Mittens, doing a little demonstration there and then.

'That's the way,' said Morgan, starting to relax. 'And don't forget, there's a final move if we need it. Anyone?'

'I know, Uncle Morgan, I know!' said a scrawny little silver cat. 'You sit down directly on top of their papers or typewriter keyboard, unsheathe your claws to start scratching and miaow your very loudest MIAOW!' She began to demonstrate a little too enthusiastically. All the others were quick to join in.

'Hush, hush, everybody! Quite right, Posy, but I don't need to hear yours or *any* cat's miaow right now.'

Morgan sighed. He really had taught them all he could. And it seemed they'd listened and learned well, despite the rocky start.

'I think you're ready,' he said. 'Okay, take the rest of the day off. Wash your whiskers and paws tonight and say your goodbyes. We're going to start placing you out tomorrow.' It was time for the final part of his plan; the trickiest to accomplish of all.

Over the previous week, in between lessons and kitten management, Morgan had made a list of all the writers coming and going through Faber and Faber's door. He of course had his favourites. Those that smelled of ink and a wood fire and anchovy spread on hot buttered toast were at the top of the list. Next came those who smelled of wild garden or warm-roofed shed. Those who smelled of *dog* had been instantly rejected.

Morgan's plan was to match the right kitten to the right author – and then smuggle them out. There was one kind-hearted but gloomy writer who always produced stories that were too long, according to Mr Eliot. Morgan thought he should take home Tom, Dick or Harry, and possibly all three. Then there was a rather highly strung poet who would benefit from the snooziest of his lap

kittens – such as Sasha or her sister, Missy. And the over-confident poet with a bombastic manner – well, she might enjoy having that little scamp Winston around the place, just the ticket to ground her . . .

Morgan spent many hours thinking it all through carefully. Only Lou-Lou's home was still undecided. She had settled down to become quite his best pupil, and he would miss her no end. It was a puzzle, but her sweetness and her spikiness didn't seem to be quite the right match for any writer he could think of.

BOOK CATS

JULY 1944

'Hello, Morgan! How *is* everybody this morning?
I was so sorry to see the bomb damage outside.
I wondered if office spirits might be raised by this
fruit cake? Will you take Mr Eliot a slice and tell
him I'm here? If he'd like to see me, that is. Oh,

I do hope my new work is worth showing him.'
The writer stepped through the door, took off
her gloves and fidgeted nervously.

Morgan was happy to take charge of the cake.
Once he'd seen the woman safely deposited in a
chair in Mr Eliot's office, he checked the coast
was clear. Yes. He silently summoned an easy-
going long-haired ginger kitten from a plant pot.

'Okay, Fitzroy, you're the first. This one is
very talented, but lacks confidence. Your loud
purr will help settle her. See her coat on the peg?
Climb up, hop in the pocket and then – *sit tight*.'

'Won't she notice, Uncle Morgy?'

'Oh no, no.' Morgan licked the kitten's ear reassuringly. 'Authors don't notice anything on their way out of here. They leave with their head full of ideas, itching to get back to their typewriter – you'll see.'

'So when do I show myself?'

Morgan paused. 'Well, you've got to trust your whiskers; it's up to you now.

You'll find the right moment. Surprise her on the train if you must, but better once she's in through her own front door. All you need to do is remember what I told you: shiver, mewl and look lost – your very biggest eyes – just how we practised.'

As Morgan predicted, half an hour after she'd gone into the office, the author drifted out, scribbling in a notebook, with her hair awry and a glazed expression on her face. She shrugged herself into her coat and gave Morgan an absent-minded stroke goodbye. Morgan's last glimpses of Fitzroy were the tips of two gingery ears poking out of the pocket and a flash of sparkling green eyes. He sighed. His part was done. Whatever

happened now, Morgan was pleased that at least one kitten was on his way to being safe out of London.

By the end of that first day the tally was up to eight. Morgan placed two kittens with a rather gruff older writer, while their braver tortoiseshell sister, who was willing to adventure alone, left with a smart lady who lived on the coast. Some kittens departed in pockets, some in briefcases and handbags, and one inside a rolled-up umbrella – Morgan kept his claws crossed that it wouldn't start to rain!

He watched the carriage clock on the mantelpiece anxiously. Once it chimed six and the last of the staff began to lock up, he relaxed. With the office closed, no one could come back with a kitten in their hands. Morgan knew that a night with a kitten would melt all but the hardest hearts.

The next day went a little less smoothly. Posy was supposed to be going home with a scruffy young author but when he started sneezing violently, Morgan knew he had to think again. He remembered his old banana-stealing days and sprang up the startled author's leg – 'OW!' – deftly retrieving Posy. He ran off before it could be spotted what he was carrying.

'Allergies . . .' Morgan explained as he dropped the kitten in an umbrella stand. 'Sorry, Posy, I didn't know. I'll find someone else even better for you, don't you worry.'

Another writer, intended for Jumble, arrived coatless and bagless. Morgan thought that he would also have to let this one leave

empty-handed. But Jumble, showing off his old affinity for heads, made a last-minute leap from the banisters on to the top of the departing author's hat.

Puzzled by the jolt, the author looked up, then shrugged and walked away, unaware that

Jumble was clinging to the hat with all his claws. The kitten waved his tail triumphantly to Morgan as the author disappeared down the street.

By the end of the week, despite a few hiccups, only one kitten remained. Lou-Lou had abandoned the teapot after her first day and had spent the week behind the tall bookshelves in Mr Faber's office. There she'd proved surprisingly quiet and well-behaved.

'So, Lou-Lou. Just you left to go now, is it?' said Morgan that evening, trying to sound casual and hearty. 'I've decided Mr Sassoon will be the author for you. I know he's got a smart country house and a young son. You'll like to be part of a

family, I reckon. And he'd be lucky to have you.'
Morgan's voice went a little growly and gruff.

'Oh yes, I've read all of
Mr Sassoon's books,' said
Lou-Lou.

'Read them? His books?'
echoed Morgan.

'Of course. What did you think I've been
doing all week? I've read everything on these
shelves. Stories are *wonderful*. I never knew how
they could take you so many places.'

'I see,' said Morgan, trying not to sound

surprised. He liked books very much – the look and the smell of them – but it had never occurred to him to actually *read* them. 'Well, Lou-Lou, I'm sure Mr Sassoon will write plenty more with your help.'

'I hope he does too, but he'll have to do it without me,' said Lou-Lou. 'I've decided I'm not going anywhere, Uncle Morgy. I like it *here*.'

Morgan bristled his tail like a bottle brush. 'Not this again. I thought you understood, Lou-Lou: you're not staying here. Not with the bombs and the risks as they are. You'll do as I say, and as your ma wanted, and leave London, you hear me? I'll not lose you. Not like I lost *my* ma and sister . . .'

Lou-Lou reached up and touched her nose gently to Morgan's. 'I'm so sorry you got left alone. But you're not going to be alone again and you won't lose me, Uncle. I've been listening to Mr Faber and the others – I've heard of a place where I'll be quite safe right here in London, one where I can use all the lessons you've taught me. I am going to be a *different* sort of Book Cat. Just you wait and see . . .'

VICTORY CAT

MAY 1945

Ding-dong, ding-dong, ding-dong! All across London
the bells were ringing out. The streets were
thronged with people laughing and crying and
hugging each other: at last the war was over.

On the rooftop of 24 Russell Square a pair of cats curled tails together and watched the partying below.

'I told you it was worth making it up here, Morgan. Tonight's a night to be up with the moon,' said a now full-grown and beautiful shiny-coated tabby cat.

'You're right, Lou-Lou. I suppose given all the rebuilding that's going to be happening, a bent drainpipe or two won't matter much.' Morgan looked guiltily at the path he'd just taken. Tonight it had taken a while for his older and better-covered bones to make the journey. He was a little out of breath.

'Don't worry about that now. We made it up here and, thanks to you, we made it through the war. That's worth celebrating, isn't it?' Lou-Lou gave him a friendly nudge.

'I suppose it is. There were times when I didn't think we would.' He paused. 'There were worse times, when I didn't much care one way or another whether I did.'

'We'll not forget those who didn't,' said Lou-Lou quietly.

Morgan gazed up at the stars. Two shone particularly bright for him. They were comforting rather than painful to see. He'd been very lucky.

His mother and sister had been two of too many Londoners who'd been horribly unlucky. But he hoped they'd be proud of him and the use he'd made of his extra lives. Twenty-three kittens moved to safety. Not to mention fourteen writers producing much better words as a result.

He had even heard the editors say so: 'Much more concise!' 'An abrupt but very welcome change of style.' 'At last! He's written the bestseller I always knew he could.' And if Morgan cleaned his whiskers with a slightly self-satisfied air after hearing them, then who could blame him?

Actual news of the kittens was hard to come by, but occasionally an author would stroke

Morgan and say something like: 'Hello, old man. No bacon rinds for you today, I'm afraid. Not now we've got a cat of our own. Turned up on our doorstep just after my last visit here, in fact. Most mysterious!' And if Morgan regretted the loss of bacon rinds, he was pleased to know his little charges were settled.

But none could make him more proud than Lou-Lou: a Book Cat to end all Book Cats, responsible not just for a single writer but for the output of *all* writers. She had found her perfect Book Cat position, looking after the underground book stores of the British Museum Library – just round the corner . . .

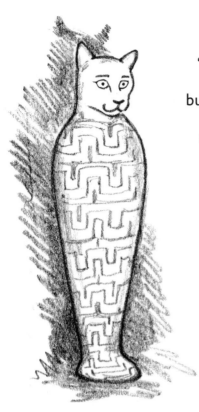

'I hear you are going to be busy, Lou-Lou,' Morgan said now.

Lou-Lou looked a little startled. 'How did you know already?'

'It's obvious. Now the war's over they'll be wanting to move all the books back. I know you've been looking after plenty down in the basements but I hear there were thousands more volumes stored in Wales, away from the bombs.'

'Oh, the *books*!' Lou-Lou curled her tail neatly round her paws. 'Don't worry, I've got everything under control and ready. The shelves are dusted, mice banished, catalogues rearranged. We librarians have been working all hours for weeks now. But I thought you were talking about something else,' she continued shyly. 'I've got a surprise to tell you, Uncle . . . I'm expecting kittens!'

Kittens! Morgan's heart swelled. 'Oh, that's *wonderful,*

Lou-Lou! Who's the daddy?' He became fierce: 'Is he treating you well? Why haven't I met him yet?'

Lou-Lou looked full-saucer-of-cream pleased with herself. 'Don't worry, Uncle Morgy, you'll meet Eisenhower later. He's *American*! Came over with the soldiers as a kitten but stuck around to work in the kitchens of the Bloomsbury Hotel. He's going to bring up a nice bit of cod for us tonight, as a matter of fact.'

'An American with cod? Well, bless my paws!' Morgan was impressed.

Lou-Lou looked shy. 'Uncle Morgan, would you mind if we named one of the kittens after you, and one after your sister?'

Morgan blinked. 'I'd be honoured,' he said gruffly.

'That's good. Because I was also wondering whether . . .' Lou-Lou started cleaning her whiskers casually, 'you might take them – to train up and place out when they're big enough? Now the war's over, I know we won't need to evacuate kittens any more but I'd like my babies to have a proper *profession*. Between my library duties and Eisenhower's hours at the restaurant we'd be grateful for some help to set them on the right path . . .'

Morgan flexed his claws while he thought. He'd been wondering what he'd do now the war was over and life would be settling back to normal. There was enough of the street cat still in him that he didn't want to get *too* fixed in his habits. But how busy did he want to be? 'A new set of kittens?'

'There are ever so many more libraries in need of a cat,' Lou-Lou continued, rubbing her cheek against Morgan's persuasively. 'And then there are booksellers and illustrators, as well as all the authors coming back from war with fresh stories. Some of those stories are going to be tough to tell; they'll need a Book Cat by their side.'

'I suppose it couldn't hurt to take on a few more,' said Morgan. It would be a shame to let all his lessons go to waste now he'd perfected them.

'That's quite settled then,' said Lou-Lou.
'Now . . . it's about time we made some music,
isn't it?' As sweet-voiced as her mother, Lou-Lou
lifted her head to caterwaul. Morgan listened to
her, his tail gently swaying with pride. He felt
tired, but happy. The war was over and Lou-Lou's
future was secure.

Morgan watched other cats climb up on to
rooftops from all over Russell Square. The streets
below were full of the voices and instruments
of people making merry. High above, the cats
were striking up their own tunes. Cats and
people, people and cats were beginning a party
that would continue through the night; a party
to celebrate a brand-new world of peace and

opportunity for all. The mix of melodies made Morgan's whiskers tingle, until at last even a grand old Book Cat of Book Cats could resist no longer. Morgan puffed out his chest and raised up his voice with Lou-Lou's. And together, the cats sang a song of joy.

AFTERWORD

ALAN: Has she finished?

BABS: I think she's still fiddling. Hasn't typed the finishing words.

ALAN: Humans! So lazy! In the time she's been

sat there, staring at the screen and chewing her nails, tapping words in and zapping them out again, some of us have been let in and out five times, shinned up six fences, climbed three trees, chased a rat, worried a frog, spilled the milk, sorted the laundry, licked two sets of ears clean and STILL managed three good snoozes.

BABS: I suppose she did have to let us out. And in. And go out for more milk. And put the laundry back in the whirly wet monster for some reason.

ALAN: It's important for her to get up from her desk. Get fresh air and fresh thoughts.

BABS: This story deserved her best work. I'm glad Morgan the Marvellous, Book Cat of Book Cats, has had his tale told at last. And that we've helped her tell it right. She's needed a few kneadings with claws when she went off track.

ALAN: She's very lucky to have us.

BABS: She is.

ALAN: But now it's getting dark and there's salmon in the fridge. Enough is enough . . .

BABS: You're right.

ALAN: Let's type the last words for her. Quick –
on to the keyboard . . .

T*&%$

        H   a!£E

                    E..,..?

                        #@N

                            D!

She'll never notice a thing.